The Snail Who Flew

Illustrated by Carme Peris

English adaptation by Paula Franklin

Silver Burdett Company
Morristown, N.J. and Agincourt, Ontario

In the woods near where the children played, many little creatures made their homes among the grass and flowers. Ladybugs, ants, snails, bumblebees, and butterflies lived happily together.

3

Everybody liked the snails. They wore their eyes on stalks and carried their houses on their backs. The yellow one was named Curly. The red one's name was Shelley.

One day two fine, fat worms crawled up and introduced themselves to Curly and Shelley.

"I'm Dot," said the blue one.

"And I'm Spot," said the orange one.

The two snails and the two worms decided to go for a stroll in the woods. But Curly soon fell behind. "I don't want this yellow house," he wailed. "It's too heavy!"

"Oh, don't be silly," scolded Shelley. "It's a beautiful home."

Another time when the four friends were playing together, two greedy birds flew up and hovered nearby. But Shelley stood her ground. "You'll have to eat my hard shell before you can get at Dot and Spot," she challenged.

The birds wanted juicy worms, not crunchy shell, so they flew away. Dot and Spot were really impressed, and thought it would be wonderful if they too could have such sturdy houses.

Several days later, the snails paid a call on their friends the worms. But Dot and Spot were nowhere to be seen. Instead two bean-shaped objects clung to some shoots of grass.

"What's happened?" asked the snails. "Are they ill? Dot and Spot have certainly changed into something strange."

14

Shelley called out to the worms, but there was no answer. "They don't move," she sobbed. "We can't play together any more."

"What stupid worms!" said Curly. "They tried to make houses like ours, and now they can't get out." He laughed, but he felt sad inside.

One day when the snails were sitting on a leaf taking it easy, two gorgeous butterflies appeared. They smiled, but the snails just stared at them.

"How have you been? Don't you remember us?" Shelley recognized Dot's voice. "Oh, it's you two," she cried. "How beautiful you've become!"

Dot and Spot had an idea. "Climb onto this leaf, Shelley, and we'll go flying."

"Can I really fly? How wonderful," exclaimed Shelley.

"I've never heard of a flying snail," muttered Curly. But he secretly yearned to try it, too.

Into the air went Shelley. Swoosh! It was like being on a magic carpet. "Wow! This is terrific!" she shouted. "The town is growing smaller and smaller!" She was full of admiration for her flying friends.

Shelley had a wonderful flight, but she didn't forget her friend Curly.

STORIES FROM
·AROUND THE WORLD·

The Snail Who Flew ©1983 Gakken Co., Ltd., Tokyo
Adapted and published in the United States by
Silver Burdett Company, Morristown, N.J.
1985 printing
ISBN 0-382-09046-2
Library of Congress Catalog Card Number 84-40800
Depósito legal: M. 8502-1985
Edime, S. A. - Móstoles (Madrid)
Printed in Spain

About the Artist

Carme Peris was born in Barcelona, Spain, where
she also attended art school. She began her
professional career as a graphic artist. Later she
went on to become an illustrator of children's books
for a number of different publishers.